THIS CANDLEWICK BOOK BELONGS TO:

_____

_____

_____

For Mom, a most dashing Pirate Queen
C. C.

To George MacDonald Fraser these pictures are humbly dedicated.
J. M.

First paperback edition 2009

The Library of Congress has cataloged the hardcover edition as follows:

Crimi, Carolyn.
Henry & the Buccaneer Bunnies / Carolyn Crimi ; illustrated by John Manders. — 1st ed.
p.   cm.
Summary: Captain Barnacle Black Ear, baddest of the Buccaneer Bunnies, is ashamed of
his book-loving son, Henry, until the day a great storm approaches.
ISBN 978-0-7636-2449-1 (hardcover)
[1. Books and reading — Fiction. 2. Pirates — Fiction. 3. Rabbits — Fiction.]
I. Title: Henry and the Buccaneer Bunnies. II. Manders, John, ill. III. Title.
PZ7.C86928He 2005
[E] — dc22   2004062936

ISBN 978-0-7636-4540-3 (paperback)

2 4 6 8 10 9 7 5 3 1

Printed in China

This book was typeset in Myriad and Blackfriar.
The illustrations were done in watercolor, gouache, and pencil.

Candlewick Press
99 Dover Street
Somerville, Massachusetts 02144

visit us at www.candlewick.com

Henry & the Buccaneer Bunnies

Carolyn Crimi

illustrated by John Manders

CANDLEWICK PRESS

Cruising the seven seas on a rickety old ship called the *Salty Carrot* sailed a wild, rowdy band of Buccaneer Bunnies.

They were bad, bad bunnies, all right. When pirates on other ships saw their long floppy ears and their fluffy white tails, they shook with fear.

The captain of the *Salty Carrot* was Barnacle Black Ear, the baddest bunny brute of all time. Black Ear was proud of his wooden paw, his golden earrings, and his mean reputation. What Black Ear was not proud of was his son, Henry.

Instead of performing his proper pirating duties, Henry was more interested in reading the books the buccaneers stole from other ships.

"Shout 'Shiver me timbers!'"
Black Ear ordered.

"I'd rather
finish this chapter,"
said Henry.

"Make this prisoner walk the plank!"

"Can't I just read about it?" asked Henry.

"Find yerself a parrot for yer shoulder!"

"First I need to read up on parrot care," said Henry.

"Buccaneer Bunnies don't need books!" said Black Ear.

"Toss 'em overboard!" he yelled to the other bunnies.

"No, wait!" cried Henry. "Let me just finish them first!"

"Avast!" cried Black Ear. "Swab the decks until ye come to yer senses!"

And so Henry swabbed the decks, day after day, while reading some of his favorite books, like *Rabbitson Crusoe* and *Thirty Days to Longer Ears*.

"Bet ye can't learn how to do this from a book!" Jean LeHare said while sharpening his hook. Henry sighed and turned the page.

"You'll never find booty like this in a book," Calico Jack Rabbit told him, holding up his stolen loot. Henry shrugged and turned the page.

"Can't do this with a book in yer paw," Bartholomew Bunny said while sanding his peg leg. Henry just turned another page.

As much as he loved his books, Henry was a lonely buccaneer bunny if ever there was one.

Then one morning, he looked up at the red sky and wriggled his little pink nose. He heard the parrots squawk and saw fish jumping out of the water.

"If my books on meteorology are correct, those signs mean a big storm is heading this way," he thought.

Henry tried telling Jean LeHare about the upcoming storm.
"Excuse me, but I believe a storm is coming," Henry said.

But Jean was too busy
polishing his pieces of eight.
"Go back to yer books,
Henry."

He tried telling Calico Jack Rabbit. "I'm pretty sure a storm is on its way," Henry said.

But Calico Jack was too busy admiring his tattoo of a cabbage.
"Don't bother me now, Henry."

Finally Henry cried,

"BATTEN DOWN
THE HATCHES!
A HUGE STORM
IS COMING!"

"What do you know about storms?" Black Ear demanded. "Get back to swabbing the deck before I make shark bait out of those books of yers!"

Henry did as he was told, but he kept his little pink eyes on the skies. When he saw the rats abandoning ship, he started packing up his books in empty treasure chests.

The storm started small. A few low grumbles of thunder. A spike of lightning. Then suddenly, a crashing, bashing, thrashing wildcat of a hurricane broke loose.

It shook the ship.

"Suffering sea dogs!"

It mangled the masts.

"Great blimey bilges!"

It slashed the sails, damaged the deck, and ripped up the rickety old *Salty Carrot.* All that was left floating on the choppy waters were a bunch of soggy bunnies and Henry's treasure chests filled with books.

When the storm finally calmed down, Black Ear, Henry, and the rest of the buccaneers paddled to the nearest island.

"**We're ruined!**" wailed Black Ear. "No ship! No pieces of eight! No gems!" He sat in the sand and blubbered like a lily-livered landlubber.

But Henry got to work.

The first thing he did was build a two-story hut out of palm fronds and coconuts.

"How did ye learn how to do THAT?" asked Black Ear.

"I read it in *101 Things to Do with Palm Fronds and Coconuts,*" replied Henry.

Next, he built a fire and cooked up a tasty seaweed stew.

"Blimey!" said the hungry bunnies. "Where did ye learn THAT?"

"I found the recipe in *Quick 'n' Easy Meals for Marooned Pirates,*" said Henry.

Then he made them all fetching garments from the bits and
pieces he had salvaged from the shipwreck.

"We look
like gentlebunnies,
we do!"

"What swank
swashbucklers we are!"

"Arr, and it's all from them landlubbin' books,"

said Black Ear, shaking his head.

Henry taught Black Ear and the Buccaneer Bunnies all kinds of useful things, like how to plant carrots,

make the best sandcastles,

and build boats out of palm fronds. Soon they built a new ship . . .

which they sailed to the library at the nearby Easter Islands every summer. Here the bunnies spent many happy hours, slurping seaweed stew and reading books.

"Aye! Buccaneer Bunnies will always need books!" said Black Ear.

Henry just smiled and turned the page.

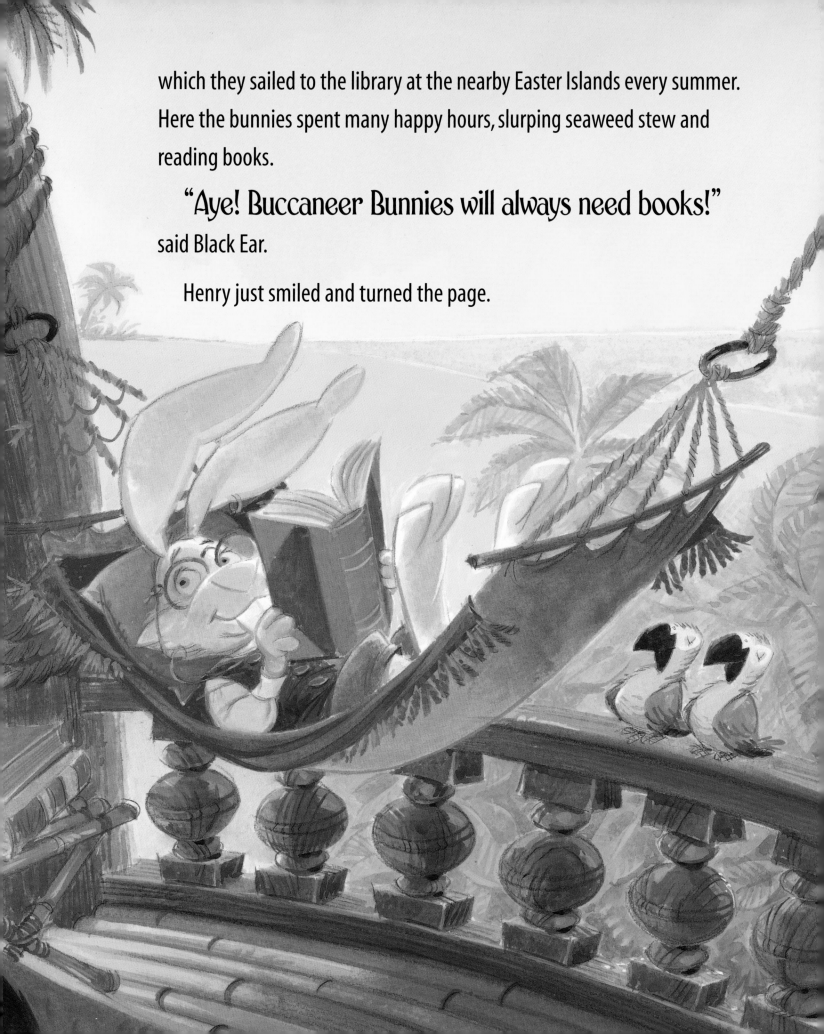

Carolyn Crimi, aka the Pirate Queen, is the author of numerous books for young readers, including *Where's My Mummy?*, illustrated by John Manders, and *Boris and Bella*, illustrated by Gris Grimly. About *Henry and the Buccaneer Bunnies*, she says, "While I don't have long floppy ears or a pronounced overbite, Henry and I are kindred spirits, who love books and carrots!" Carolyn Crimi lives in Illinois.

John Manders —thief, pirate, rogue, and children's book artist— has illustrated several picture books for children, including *Where's My Mummy?* by Carolyn Crimi, *The Perfect Nest* by Catherine Friend, and *Minnie's Diner: A Multiplying Menu* by Dayle Ann Dodds. He says, "I began my nautical career with my faithful parrot, Sherman, plundering merchantman and man-o'-war alike. From piracy, it was a small step to children's book publication." Today John Manders lives in Pennsylvania, far from the ocean's beckoning waves.